Becka and the Big Bubble

Becka goes to India

by **Gretchen Schomer Wendel and Adam Anthony Schomer**

Illustrated by Damon Renthrope

www.bbbubble.com

for Brent, Benjamin, and Dave

ISBN 978-1-933754-13-0

Printed in China

Waterside Press

Becka and the Big Bubble
PO Box 230437
Encinitas, CA 92023-0437

www.bbbubble.com or www.BeckaAndTheBigBubble.com

Becka closed her eyes

And imagined what to do

She blew and blew and **blew** and **blew...**

Flippity-Free!
This time she blew a double

To far away INDIA
Flew Becka and the Big Bubble!

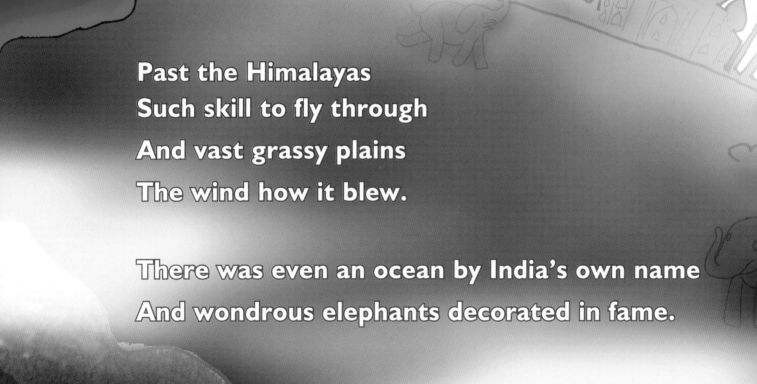

Past the Himalayas
Such skill to fly through
And vast grassy plains
The wind how it blew.

There was even an ocean by India's own name
And wondrous elephants decorated in fame.

Mumbai* is full of people

As far as one can see

"Nobody here

Looks quite like me!"

"What's that they're burning?

Crazy cool smell."

That incense is hot

POP and she fell.

*Mumbai (mum-bī), formerly known as Bombay, is India's largest city.

Gliding through the air
Becka now fell

Caught by new friends
Their secrets they'd tell.

She rode on an elephant, as a welcomed new friend

She saw in their smiles, this was not pretend.

To the Taj Mahal, a place built out of love

Smoothly carved marble, as white as a dove.

Onto Jaipur*, the lovely pink city

Hand crafted pots and carpets so pretty.

Up on the rooftops, kids flying kites

Dotting the skies, some colored some white.

*Jaipur (jī-pôr) is known for its celebration of India's kite festival.

After the kite festival
It was time to eat
"Yippidi-Dee
This looks so neat!"

Inside of the home
A feast to come soon
Yet she saw no chairs
Not even a spoon.

This culture is different, some eat with their hands

And then Becka thought..."THIS IS MY KIND OF LAND!"

She dipped bread in dips, dips they call Dahl

Each ever more spicy, Becka tried them all.

Next a Hindu wedding, bride and groom seated
Showered with gifts, as their guests came and greeted.

Laughing and loving, for days this can last
"A three day party, that sounds like a blast!"

That bald man is noble
"Who's he?" Becka asked.
"Gandhi," they said
Their smiles so vast.

He fought for the people
He fought without fists
He's one fine fellow
The world does miss.

And as if to answer
The music began
From behind the wall
To hear, Becka ran.

Beats from the Tabla, a wet sounding drum
The Sitar is relaxing like a sweet guitar's hum.

Both of these sounds native to this land
Becka closed her eyes to feel the band.

Then all of her friends danced in delight
Becka now felt how music takes flight!

Together they **blew music bubbles** in tune
Becka floated off towards the glorious moon.

"Good-bye India, a beautiful land
I hope to come back to a country so grand."

And before she knew it she could see Mom and Dad
"Pop on in, time for supper I'm glad."

Pippity-Pop!

With the flick of her nail
To the ground she sailed...

What a day it had been!

Watch and listen to
Becka online

Your free animated
video Podcast

www.bbbubble.com